Christine

Kind regards

Richard Stuart

About the Author

Richard Stuart draws on a vast experience as soldier, policeman, local politician, company director and charity worker to weave fascinating anecdotes out of our ordinary lives – is it you he details? Married with a tribe of children and grandchildren, he lives in the Midlands.

Dedication

To my inspiration – Nicola

Richard Stuart

NO WORRIES

AUSTIN MACAULEY
PUBLISHERS LTD.

A CIP catalogue record for this title is available from the British Library.

ISBN 978 1 78455 592 4 (Paperback)
ISBN 978 1 78455 593 1 (Hardback)

www.austinmacauley.com

First Published (2015)
Austin Macauley Publishers Ltd.
25 Canada Square
Canary Wharf
London
E14 5LB

Printed and bound in Great Britain

CONTENTS

MARIGOLD

You would have to say that Marigold is not the most common name for a pony; not perhaps the most obvious sort of name for a pony which was not really particularly pretty. Pretty, Marigold was not! But what he lacked in pretty he more than made up for in strength, courage, kindness and quirk. What, you may ask, is quirk? – Read on.

Marigold lived in a field almost the shape of a triangle; it was too large to be called a paddock and not large enough to be termed a prairie. It had a sort of shelter or shed in one corner which shielded Marigold from light showers but didn't really provide much cover in autumn gales and winter storms; but Marigold was tough. There was also a byre against one of the fences and another one in the middle of the field to take hay or straw or swedes or mangel-wurzels, or any other good stuff that he liked. Because of his legs and smallish hooves, horsey people thought that he had been a riding pony, maybe had won few minor events. No one knew if he had a pedigree or anything about him, because he had certainly been saddle trained, but he never let on; he was terse, reclusive, shy.

No one seemed to know who owned Marigold – there wasn't anyone in particular who came regularly to see him or care for him or groom him; he was just there. The fields were part of an enormous land holding owned by a firm based in Glasgow and it was too small and too misshapen to be ploughed by big machines, so a local tenant farmer occasionally put some hay in one of the byres and sometimes used the field for a few days for transiting lambs, but apart from that Marigold was his own master.

Unbeknown to whoever his owners were, Marigold had organised a much-loved child riding scheme: kids would come through the fence – some as young as four, and needing to be helped up – and climb on his back and off he would go on a leisurely circuit of his empire. He could, without difficulty, take four at a time. When he had completed a circuit to and from his shed he would stop, not unlike a bus waiting for passengers to get off and on; if there was no weight on his back he would move away to graze. If too many had mounted he would stand immobile, no matter how many 'Giddyups'; similarly, if an adult climbed aboard, 'No thank you'. All of this without saddle, martingale or bridle! For reward he clearly appreciated carrots, apples, celery, nuts (not salted), crisps, pulled grass, dandelions and ginger nut biscuits. His appetite was quite insatiable and he had been known to consume over thirty small to medium apples in less than one hour from grateful passengers. With some reasoning, not easily understood, Marigold had devised a 'Not In Service' signal to potential passengers. When he was indisposed, he backed his hindquarters into the hedge and always into the same yard of hedge so that it was impossible to mount. And there he would remain, calmly viewing his would-be riders, his demeanour clearly saying: "Not now folks, not quite up to it."

At another corner of his domain, a couple of gardens were separated from him by only a low wall topped by a chain. They had erected bird feeders, one of which was an iron post with arms, hooks and tray. Marigold was a naturalist, always keen to help other creatures, domestic and wild. There were a great number of pheasants in the woods around Marigoldia, always shouting and avid to share any food source he had. If ever his fans fed him nuts, a squadron of pheasants would immediately dive. On the bird feeder post, the tray was filled each evening with peanuts, apples and crusts; as soon as dawn broke, Marigold's head poked over the chain to feast on the tray fare; by so doing he jolted the post so that a cascade of peanuts and seeds from all of the bird feeders fell in a blizzard – instantly the squawking squadron dived – 'Alleluia Marigold.'

One cold winter week there had been exceptionally heavy rain and a number of the Dads of Marigold's riders got timber, plastic sheeting and roofed and extended his shack into a half-decent shelter. That it was needed and appreciated was made clear by Marigold's disappearance from view. The rain was followed by four inches of snow in one night, drifting to over two feet. Because of the rain the usual pastures were underwater and in some desperation the tenant farmer and his dogs pushed twenty-four snow-dazed sheep into Marigoldia which, being slightly higher up, had snow but no water on the ground. At gone eight the next morning, the folk looking out of their windows were astonished to see that the quirky pony had lodged almost all the sheep inside his shelter while he stood – tail against the gate – outside.

In the following spring, the sheep, or most of them, returned to Marigold's field in lamb and, over the next twelve to fifteen days, delivered: some single, two triplet but most twin lambs. Because of the woods and wide open back area, foxes are a plague and lambing always attracts Britain's No 1 not so cute semi-wild animal, which will gladly take anything on offer. Marigold was to be seen, night and day, snorting, neighing, stamping – keeping foxes running and never letting them settle, the sheep very clearly seeing him as an ally and showing no discomfort at his physical presence.

Approximately twenty miles south of our field was the British Centre for Hot Air Balloons, and every year an enormous festival took place at which balloons and balloonists planet-wide would have gathered over the week prior. The balloons, in addition to the normal onion shape, came as telephone kiosks, motor cars, airships, teapots, computers, but all vast and gaudily coloured. When fully expanded each was over thirty feet high and the roar from their gas cylinders could be heard a mile away on a mild day. The balloons are largely at the mercy of the prevailing wind and on this particular day the wind was from the south and a strong breeze. Some hour or so after lift-off the first balloons were many miles north of launch site and beginning to exhaust their gas cylinders; so their pilots were looking for suitable landing sites, free of water and electricity pylons and roads.

With the acute hearing of horses, Marigold had begun to hear a strange roaring sound behind the far barns, some five minutes earlier. He paused grazing, saw nothing, perceived no danger, resumed. The noise was now loud and yes, threatening – he was used to jet liners, he was used to choppers, farmers crop sprayed all the time in them; the police chopper had a hangar only four miles away; so it wasn't that noise.

"Oh my hooves and hide! Whatever is that, I don't like it."

A huge telephone kiosk, thirty feet high with an enormous basket hanging underneath was over his head, ROARING. It was dropping on his head! He fled in panic round and round and round – ears back, eyes out, jumping, splaying, neighing, tail everywhere! Poor, poor Marigold! The roaring stopped, the telephone kiosk fell over in a canvas heap; two men got out of the basket and stood looking at Marigold. He looked back – men, he could cope with them.

He came right up to them direct – invited them to look at his teeth with his head stretched out towards them; they moved back, moved up close again, they moved back until their backs were against the basket. And there they stayed until the young farmer and their back-up crew arrived forty minutes later. Well, Marigold thought: "Hadn't been introduced, noisy, ill-mannered; I'll just ignore them and get back to my house until they've taken that thing and themselves off."

As no one knew his name, he had been 'The Horse With No Name' for a while until one little girl who had grown very fond of him, Lucy McNeill, one day came by to give him some cashew nuts. His mane and forelock were so matted that she scurried home and quietly borrowed her big sister Megan's steel comb. The pony came back over again looking for more cashews and stood still as she gently combed out his forelock and plaited the coarse horsehair just like her own plait. When she'd finished she poked an orange marigold right into the plaited hair so that it shone like an orange star amid the dark bay hide and coal black hair. Immediately it caught on – everyone who saw the flower before it wilted next day said: "Marigold – that's his name." And so it was and so it is – MARIGOLD.

BROKER

Prentiss thought last night had been great; nice bar, couple of glasses of decent wine, smart girls, fair old banter with the boys, met a new guy with a decent sense of piss-taking, then the show not that bad and home by midnight.

Today – rubbish! Everything that could go down, down. Razor packed up – stand by emergency blade rusty – banged little toe on door and blood everywhere, no Plasters, toilet roll wrapped round cut, can't get it into shoe – drive to supermarket one shoe on and one sock, step in puddle with sock foot – leave briefcase at home – miss train. Now on later train, no seats, standing, whole bloody foot throbbing – feel like and am complete bloody idiot.

"Ouch."

"Oh, sorry."

"No problem," thinks: "Why not stand on the bloody toe again mate?"

At last in the office, sympathy surely – Janet: "Silly idiot, get a cat to kick, they're softer." Ivor: "Yeah, I thought you were going it a bit last night," etc., etc. "Shall I tread on the other one?"

Prentiss rang Jane. "Hi babe, yeah, great last night, think you'd have enjoyed it. How was your mum – oh, that good; oh dear. Are we on tonight? OK, see you at mine around seven – great, bye."

Working as an insurance broker each day was full on from 0845 until whatever time he managed to leave – twenty-hour days were common, lunch most uncommon and very few of the brokers were over forty-five. Unusually, there were almost as many women as men, probably even more aggressive; it seemed the women went the extra yard and their results were formidably good. At every social gathering it was noticeable who drove the high-end vehicles – since last year's figures had been published one young woman had begun to be seen in a Masa – the men had suffered a huge ego shock. And Lydia Sparks was now universally known as Masa. Two consecutive poor quarters and people tended not to be around.

Prentiss was in the top fifteen per cent but preferred to put his high earnings into property rather than fashion, wheels and entertainment. Already he had bought three terraced properties in Nottingham, which, with a freelance brickie, he had converted into three four-room student accommodations. Rented through the university they were as risk-free as it was possible to find and each gave him a healthy profit and the option to reinvest in more of the same. The student population was not predicted to drop any time soon. Additionally, he had been able to afford the mortgage on his three-bedroomed flat in pleasant suburbs where he now lived.

He had set himself a target of retiring from working for brokers by his fortieth year and setting up his own brokerage linked to property rental and maintenance in university cities and he had already made a fair start.

Prentiss was seen by the senior management as a very acceptable employee – responsible, diligent and effective, he always achieved targets, worked within agreed parameters and needed only notional supervision. He was earmarked for promotion although his immediate boss was reluctant to lose his guaranteed financial input to the team as a senior broker.

At the start of the week following his toe smack, Alan Mayling, his boss, said: "Prentiss, on Friday 17th Eric

Spatz would like you to come a meeting with me and him –
10.30 if that's all right, in his office – any problems with
that?"

"Hold on Alan, what's this about?"

"No worries, Prentiss, all good I promise you, we just
want to have a discussion about company plans – OK,
Friday this week, 10.30."

"Yes, fine – I'll be there."

Prentiss was, of course, intrigued and quite excited –
Eric Spatz, the General Manager, did not normally speak
with brokers except at social functions and as he knew his
results were routinely good he could not imagine the
interview would be negative; but...

Jane Oliver and her friend Theo Rayner owned a hair and
nail boutique in the middle of Pennyland, the shopping
arcade to the west of the city. Theo was gay and
delightfully happy, sociable and amusing – everyone, but
everyone was the target of Theo's non-stop banter. All men
were "Darling" and all women were "Mate" and to stand
back and see the reaction of first timers into Blush Beauty
when addressed by Theo as such was itself both opera and
comedy. Everyone also was embraced at some time in their
visit by the highly perfumed, exquisitely made up and
divinely dressed Theo! How could Blush Beauty possibly
fail? – it couldn't; Jane was an excellent cutter and a hard-
headed businesswoman and they employed only talented
Thai nail artists and good hair colourists. Theo could do
anything to do with hair – well; he had ongoing feuds with
his Thai employees about the length and colour of his own
personal acrylics!

Between them the business flew.

When Jane and Prentiss met there were number of hot
topics – who would start? Of course, Jane: "Darling, Theo
has been giving me grief as much as Theo could ever give

me grief; he wants to speak to you professionally about investing his money. I've explained to him twenty times that you handle only corporate business but he goes all silly and pretends he is a business and all that garbage – can you handle it once and for all honey?"

"Sure, I'll sort it."

"Thanks babe, I've seen a great bargain in Wood Street Motors. I want you to look at it."

"Yeah, what's that?"

"It's an unusual dark green Ferrari – it's £78k and I thought what an investment to hold for say five years and sell on – I don't mean drive it, what do you think?"

"Not much sweetheart, but I'll look."

"Great babe – have you thought any more about getting married? I really want a baby, darling!"

"Sweetheart, hold on, this is all new stuff – we decided at Christmas that we would not get married for at least two years and kids were not in the frame. You can't just go Ferrari, marry, kids all in one serve."

"Well that's not all sweetie, I'm considering whether I should open a second branch and whether we should buy some property in Tobago."

"Jane, I need to think – first up, I'll talk to Theo!"

Over the next three days, Prentiss had a particularly stressful time – the second largest brokerage deal he had ever landed, died, resurrected, died and finally landed, causing him severe stress, worry and commercial angst; the meeting with Spatz had taken place – he had been told he was to head up a new high-risk, foreign-trading, London-based venture which would mean much absence from the UK. Highly paid, but enormously difficult, and no choice – yes or goodbye.

His partner needed to be gently persuaded that her future lay with him, even though she would not often see him, that they were not to be married soon, that he would not impregnate her, that he did not wish to garage her Ferrari and he thought property in Trinidad risky; further, as the main reason for the success of her business was the permanent joint presence of she and Theo, their guaranteed absence from a second branch…

Could any future week possibly be as fraught?

NATALIE'S GARDEN

At the bottom of the garden they'd planted hornbeams, five of them – fastigiate the shape, like an upside down wine glass, to cut out the view of the large house beyond. They were just fifteen feet high, the saplings, and they planted them on top of at least two feet of manure and bonemeal additive. Now, eight years later, the garden had matured nicely and the hornbeams were over thirty feet high, sentinels keeping out the unwanted sight of bricks and chimneys. Both Robert and Natalie loved their garden and spent lots of hours there, shaping and digging and cutting and planting and working and loving.

When first they moved in they had downsized – the children had grown up and away and they'd decided to take tedious labour out – so the garden was a grass-free zone. Sold the mowers and strimmers and edgers and had a marvellous time choosing gravel – size, shape, colour; and pots – so many beautiful, beautiful pots; earthenware, ceramic, pot, clay, china, glass, bronze, alloy, wicker, wood, stone – so many beautiful pots and such wonderful fun choosing, buying, changing mind, disagreeing, choosing again, awaiting delivery, siting them, moving them, moving again, filling them, planting them, replanting them – grass? Are you mad? – NEVER SUCH FUN WITH GRASS!!!!!

Robert loved figs – he loved figs all his life in any way you could get figs – after years of bombardment, Natalie gave way, as long as it wasn't to take over. "You know figs take over everything."

Robert went to three nurseries and spoke to the RHS – they all said the same: "Starve them or all you'll get is leaves." "Which variety?" "Oh, for a smallish garden – Brown Turkey."

So he bought a very large 36-inch diameter pot and, to starve the fig tree, blocked up all the base holes bar one. As its roots could, therefore, not take over the garden, it would produce fruit whilst living in its large pot. And after two years, so it did; lovely green then brown, large, luscious figs; and all he did was water it with dilute fertilizer and put an old car cover over it November to April.

Meantime, Natalie had been steadily constructing perfect flower beds, enclosing the gravel rectangle within its gently coloured barge boards. Architectural stipa grasses, pampas grass in pots, hybrid highly scented roses in damask shades of carmine and rose and pink, paeonies, begonias, dahlias, geraniums, pelargoniums, delphiniums, nigella, mollis, scabious.

In her herb pots – thyme, dill, coriander, more thyme, camomile, rosemary, parsley, sage, oregano, tarragon.

The scent from mid-May to early November was paradise. The hornbeams had become avian tenement blocks – because Natalie and Robert were keen to watch and protect birds they had cat-proofed the garden, put up eleven different bird feeders, kept them full and watched. Birds rapidly realised how safe and productive the garden was and came throughout the year – robins, sparrows, dunnocks, wrens, blackbirds, starlings, rooks in winter – in spring and summer, twenty four different species.

In the hornbeams, there appeared to be a strict nesting protocol – blackbirds in the bottom tier about fifteen feet from ground; sparrows and dunnocks next up, about twenty feet up, above them greenfinch, chaffinch and tits and at the very top forty feet plus, goldfinches. The months of May and June kept Robert busy chasing magpies away from eggs and unfledged chicks – he won some, but sadly, not all.

"Robert, I don't like our raised bed, can we get rid?"

"Darling, it's been there less than two years and was exactly what you wanted."

"Yes, I know, but I'm not happy with it."

"There's more than four tonnes of top soil, two rose arbours and nearly two tonnes of sleepers to get rid of."

"I know, darling."

"What do you want in its place?"

"A water feature, darling"

"Of course, darling. What else could you possibly…"

And so it came to pass – the water feature is a globe of striated golden sandstone, hollow in the centre, atop a large reservoir (hidden underground) and recirculating pump. It looks striking and the water bubbling over the top down over rocks to the hidden reservoir sounds peaceful and endless. Robert sometimes wonders if it will one day be replaced by a replica of the sphinx.

Lots and lots of people come to Natalie's and Robert's house on one pretext or another and either sit in the conservatory or on the benches in the garden – they can calm down in the gentle water burble or watch anything up to thirty-five feeding birds or smell roses and honeysuckle or mollis or lavender or just look at the beautiful trees and shrubs and flowers.

Probably, from one visit to the next, Natalie will have planted something new or replanted something old or just asked Robert to paint a bench a different colour. You'll feel welcome.

THE RING

At the time of his birth, William Iscot Grant was promised by his godfather, John Grant, a serviette ring. William, being rather small at the time, knew nothing of this but his mother, Elizabeth, John's sister-in-law, made the appropriate noises and thought no more about it. A year later, the family decided to have the little boy christened, mainly because William's grandparents kept on and on and on about tradition and 'always been done' and on the day, John Grant produced a solid silver, six-sided, oblong serviette ring – each end v-shaped.

Tiny William was photographed holding it; it was then reboxed and James Grant, his father and John's brother, said: "Johnnie, many thanks; will you get it engraved W.I.G.?"

"Of course I will, James, I just wanted to be sure that was what you wanted.

"Thanks Johnnie – we'll leave it with you then."

On William's fifth birthday, Johnnie came to the party; he'd been in Argentina for several years. James greeted him: "Hi Johnnie, where's it gone?"

"What d'you mean?"

"The serviette ring – where's it gone?"

"Oh my word – it must be at Aitkens, you know, the jewellers, where I bought it. I took the ring back to be engraved after the christening and what with packing and leaving – Oh my word, I'm mortified – Elizabeth, I'm so sorry."

"So you should be; some present to your godson, he got it for thirty seconds then bosh, it's gone."

"I'll call them right away; can I use your phone? I've left my cellphone somewhere."

Surprisingly, the serviette ring was retrieved from Aitkens, now duly engraved W.I.G. and as Elizabeth astutely commented, this really is the "Where's It Gone" ring.

Just after William's eighth birthday, Grandma Grant rang.

"Is that you, William?"

"Yes Grandma, how are you?"

"I'm fine, thank you, William, I'm calling to ask if you would like to come and stay with me and Grandpa for a wee while."

"What, up in Scotland?"

"Yes, William, up here in the wilds of Scotland – I've already spoken to your mum and she says it's fine with her, so what do you think?"

"I'd love to come Grandma – when will that be?"

"I'll arrange it with your parents, but soon, bye bye for now."

"Bye, Grandma."

Williams stayed a week and, being proud of his serviette ring, it stayed too.

Grandpa taught him to fish and Grandma to bake and they admired his serviette ring at every meal. John arrived at the end of the stay to bring his son home to find turmoil – packing complete but the ring was missing.

"Where's it gone?"

John waited over an hour before saying to his very upset son: "Grandpa and Grandma will find it and send it to you but we must go now."

They had search and searched and searched!

Two days later, the manager of the Salvation Army shop in Perth rang Mr Grant senior: "Good morning, is that Mr Grant, this may be a wild goose chase sir, I'm Ian McNair of the Salvation Army and our van collected a bag of clothes from your house and other houses in your area this week. Are you missing anything of value?"

"Indeed I am, Mr McNair; is it an item of silver?"

"It is, sir, can you tell me what you are missing?"

"We're missing what we call the 'Where's It Gone' serviette ring – a six-sided serviette ring engraved W.I.G. made of sterling silver."

"Well, Mr Grant, it would seem we may have the item here if you would come to reclaim it from our shop here."

"I'll be down within the hour; and can you tell me how you identified us as the possible owners?"

"Aye, I can, one of our helpers, Mrs McLeod, was shown the ring by, I think, your grandson when she was having tea in your house last week – a happy occurrence I would say."

Registered mail returned W.I.G. to a delighted William. Years passed, W.I.G. acquired the patina of used silver. William prepared to depart for his first term at uni; soccer boots, books, toiletries, W.I.G. – oh, no, where's it gone?

"When did you last use it?" asked Elizabeth.

"Not sure, hmm, probably last Christmas."

"Did you put it back?"

"Can't remember, but why wouldn't I; oh no, remember? We had the Boltons staying and they helped clear away after Christmas dinner, so it could have gone anywhere – damn."

"W.I.G. has a life of its own. You should know that by now; it'll turn up." Disgruntled, William departed to uni.

John and Elizabeth had been discussing downsizing for years and now that William had departed, (and, pragmatically, they knew he wouldn't ever live at home again) they did the deed.

Just eighteen miles away, they needed to compress into two bedrooms and box, so lots of furniture had to go – heartache time. They agreed what would stay and Elizabeth fled to her sister's while John got through the trauma of disposal and removal. To go was an old oak sideboard with such wonky drawers that they'd ceased using them a decade ago – a last check. John wrenched one open and the front with handle broke off; he got a claw hammer and prised out he sides and back and there was W.I.G. – where a Bolton must have thrown it, not knowing not to use the drawer.

The box bedroom was William's should he ever be home – Elizabeth suggested to him that W.I.G. might be safer there than in student accommodation and so in a box above the bed he lurked. At uni William, over three years, acquired the usual phalanx of acquaintances but also four friends who each owned silver birth serviette rings. Despite misgivings, he took W.I.G. to uni in his last year and photographed for posterity five friends dining with their five birth tokens.

In his mid-twenties he married one of the friends, Isla, and of course their places at the wedding breakfast included their serviette rings – because they had just exchanged wedding rings, they thought it symbolic to do the same at the table; so W.I.G. was at Isla's place setting around her pale blue serviette, complementing her palest blue gown. The wedding breakfast was a delight and come speech time everyone keenly anticipated William's response to Isla's father's encomium. His climax was the symbol of 'our two wedding rings, and even our two birth-given serviette rings' and as he stooped to scoop them up 'W.I.G.' – the curse had struck again. Embarrassed – "I'll finish there, thanks everyone once again, see you all soon."

"Where on earth has it gone, darling, they were both here, side by side, fifteen minutes ago."

Dale, his best man, came in. "The caterers cleared everything into bags, Will – it must be in one of those. I'll go."

"Thanks Dale, please, please find it." And after an hour or more and much ill-feeling from the caterers, who did not want to sift through fifteen bags of rubbish – they did.

Just after William's twenty-ninth birthday, Isla and he, surrounded by clan and chums, met in the grounds of Dorland Park for a party to celebrate the birth of their first child, Catherine. There were lots and lots of them and they thought it a lovely gesture when William, in a little speech, dedicated his W.I.G. serviette ring to his daughter, adding that Isla and he could share hers.

Time to go after a lovely, lovely day, all packed up – "Who's got it?" "What?" "You know, W.I.G!"

CONSEQUENCES

The house had been empty for several months – the young owner, Henry, had been promoted by his company and moved to Portsmouth.

"I'm not going to sell it because they're paying for my accommodation for a year and I'll see what happens," he'd said.

Now someone had leased it and Rachel and Iain next door were glad it was to be occupied. Henry came back for a day.

"He's an older chap, a writer, I think, seemed decent enough and he's taken it for two years initially; his name's Peter Wheatley, if I give you my number, could you call me if you see something silly? You know what I mean – thanks a million, I'll be in touch."

Peter Wheatley moved in directly and Iain went round, as neighbours do. "Hi, I'm Iain, anything you need to know, anything we can do, we're at No 16 and here's my cell number."

"Well that's very kind; I'm Peter Wheatley. I think I'm OK so far but I'll shout if I need to. Hold on a moment and I'll give you my card." Iain couldn't help but notice that Peter had severe problems walking, and from his card learned he was a writer and commercial journalist.

Iain thought he could collect and return Peter's four recycling bins on the days they were due – it would be almost impossible for Peter. And so he did, anonymously, over the next few months before Peter was able to find out who the Samaritan was, through a chance remark by another neighbour. On the day that, Peter's sister, Susan, happened to be visiting he said: "I've only just learned that it's you I have to thank for moving my bins in and out; I'm extremely grateful."

"Please don't mention it, I'm doing mine at the same time."

"Well, I can't tell you how grateful I am – are you off out?"

"Yes, I've got to find some goats' milk for Rachel, my wife, she has a type of asthma which is intolerant of cow dairy products, so she uses goat alternatives; and the shop which has always supplied us has changed hands and doesn't stock it now."

"Well, how extraordinary," said Peter. "Susan, let me introduce her, my sister, runs a herd of goat milkers, I'm sure she..."

"Yes, of course, I'd be delighted to help," said Susan. "My place is only eight miles away; shall I speak to your wife now?"

"Yes, please that would be a big help."

"See you later, Peter, this way Susan."

And so a direct consequence of one good turn...

While Susan and Rachel were arranging a regular supply of goats' milk, Susan's cell phone rang.

"Excuse me, Rachel. Hello, Susan speaking, yes I am the goat breeder, nice to speak to you too; I'm out of my office, could you call me on this number in an hour so we can talk further? OK, fine. Rachel, I must fly – more business, really nice to meet you and do business, bye."

Susan's phone caller had been a senior veterinarian lecturer from Liston Agricultural College who wanted to set up a regular programme of visits for his students to a live goats' milk dairy unit. The college had been unable for a considerable time to find a suitable field partner for one of its advanced courses.

In the same week: "Welcome Dr Jerrold – in principle I'm not against becoming involved in an education programme, but I must emphasise that primarily we are a commercial operation."

"May I ask what you do?"

"There are two prime aims: to breed goats and to produce and sell goats' milk products commercially."

After a lengthy discussion, they agreed to a regular programme of student team visits over the next eighteen months. Dr Jerrold was visibly relieved and delighted – a fee was agreed and as a token of gratitude he offered free of charge its veterinary care for the goat herd; a considerable saving of expenditure and yet another consequence of a good turn.

On his return from Susan's farm, Dr Jerrold took a minor country road narrow, winding and bordered with dense, high hedges. Windows down, he approached the first dwelling he had seen, a thatched cottage; a muntjac deer jumped out of the nearside hedge immediately in front, causing him to swerve violently to the right. His car hit the cottage wall, smashing his headlight and by some freak a sliver of glass streaked up through his open window, embedding in his right wrist. It gashed the artery and he immediately poured blood everywhere. Shocked by the bang of the impact, a woman ran out of the cottage door, took one look and ran back – reappearing immediately with a medical kitbag. By this time Jerrold was going into shock with heavy blood loss. Cutting the sleeves of his jacket and shirt and laying him back she extracted the glass sliver, applied a tourniquet and put an emergency dressing on the wound. In four minutes he was stabilised. Crashing outside a paramedic's home, yet another consequence…?

TABLE TALK

When they looked back on it they had difficulty remembering exactly how it had all started. You know, the Table Talk. The venue was always the same, Jim and Alison's back garden, or if it rained, the conservatory with its veranda and overhang; it depended on how hard it was raining. They didn't seem to do it after October end. There was Alison and Jim and Tom and Celia and Andrew and Benedicta and Derek and Francis. Derek and Francis were a couple but not married but they argued like a married couple, so it was fine.

And all they did was come through the back gate about 10am most weekday mornings and sit down around the table and talk. There were two tables – one a painted wooden, fold-up, lattice contraption and the other a large, round, white metal job which also folded if you wished and had three white matching chairs. Jim thought the third had been left by someone years ago but he wasn't bothered. No one had a 'mine' chair so you could mingle, and they did.

Andrew had the remains of a Scottish accent and liked to shout phrases 'D'you ken' but what followed was Midlands. His wife, Benedicta, was a Filipina, petite, dark, charming and utterly unable to pronounce the letter F so that she addressed Derek's partner invariably as 'Prancis' to everyone's amusement and delight.

"Who's for tea and who's not please?' was Alison's greeting by 10.15 each day – those arriving after the others had been 'mugged' had to make their own in her kitchen.

Now and again, someone would give Jim a couple of quid with thanks as milk money.

Table talk had become a regular in their lives to which they all set the days' rhythms. All retired, most of them early, all great neighbours originally and now elevated into friends, it was almost a family because so much talk had revealed so many private and a few secret details of all and each of them.

"Derek and me, we're thinking of a steamer trip around the Outer Hebrides in autumn; we wondered if anyone's interested. We've done a bit of research."

After a break, Tom said: "Celia and I might, only might be; we were talking last week about a late UK hol, weren't we?"

"Yes, what sort of money per person per week, Francis?"

"Varies a bit on cabin etc., but a rough guide would be £700 per week plus fares up to Scotland and back."

"Alison," asked Benedicta, "have you had problems with snails since you planted out your dahlias?"

"No snails, B, but rotten slugs the length of my finger, have given me a real nightmare."

"What's your defence, Alison?" asked Derek.

"I've tried most things, salt, pellets, you name it, but dew and rain just dissolve them and you're back to where you were."

"There's a waterproof pellet on the market now, bit more expensive but it doesn't wash away so that might sort it for you," said Tom.

Celia: "Tom have you got the new book on car prices, I think you said it was coming out this week."

"Yes, I got it on Monday; are you getting a new car?"

"Don't know, we think something about eighteen months old might be good, perhaps a Mazda."

"Right, I'll go and fetch it, you can have it for a couple of days."

"Thanks Tom, I'll bring it back before Friday."

"That's fine."

Andrew asked Derek: "Why are you thinking of the Western Isles, Derek, have you been before?"

"No, I've not, Andrew, but I've always wanted to go and I've got a lot of brochures and articles and pictures which show just how beautiful it is, islands, the sea, beaches, cliffs, you know, marvellous; have you ever been?

"No, never, but like you I wish to and hope some day we will."

Benedicta interrupted: "Excuse me everyone, Alison and I are going to the cinema on Thursday afternoon – is anyone else interested? There's a choice of six films and it's nine pounds – I've got the programme here if you want to see."

Eventually six decided to go and did – a re-run of *The Outlaw Josey Wales*.

At 12.10 only Jim was left, until they all started talking around the table again next day – nice.

THE OLD POND

In the hamlet, that was mentioned in the Domesday Book, there had always been a pond. A great-grandfather remembered shooting snipe on it back in the 1920s, when things were quite a bit less caring. The pond was hidden under the high hawthorn trees at the entrance and was very easy to miss. Now the hamlet had become a village in the government's housing development, out in the country and therefore very desirable; affluent, large properties, quiet closes, wide lawns, parkways and roundabouts.

The Parish Council had always been anonymous, same chairman for forty years, his wife, a deaf retired postman and two vacancies. Now it had a population of six hundred instead of thirty-seven and one hundred and four vehicles instead of eleven to administer. Suddenly, parish council meetings saw members of the public – unprecedented.

"Good evening chairman, do you take questions at the start or end of meetings? I'm Gareth Clark, 14 Farm View," was the first question asked in thirty-one years.

"Er, at the end, I suppose," responded Joseph Binks, the chairman, retired teacher.

At the end of the meeting, which was ten minutes later, Gareth Clark again: "Thank you Chair, I should like to know what is the mechanism for Parish Council elections. What is the constitution of the council, when are elections held, how many vacancies are there currently?"

"Well, Mr Clark, this is the Annual General Meeting, the council comprises five members, there are currently two vacancies and anyone who resides in the village who is eighteen or over and is of sound mind may nominate anyone similar if four weeks' notice is given prior to the AGM. Nominations to fill vacancies may be made at any time."

"Thank you Chair, my name is Rowena Ledger of 23 Field End, I would like to know, was the AGM advertised and does the Parish Council have an obligation to advertise it?"

"Thank you Ms Ledger – the answer is no it was not advertised nor has it ever been advertised and I don't know whether we have to advertise it or not."

"Good evening Chairman my name's John Baker from 17 Field End – it seems to me that an AGM cannot be valid if the voters for whom it is held are not told it is being held, or when or where; further, as far as I know, there has not been any publicity to invite applications for the post of councillor, nor to fill the existing vacancies."

"Mr Chair, Gareth Clark again – can you tell us how long has each vacancy existed?"

"Well, ladies and gentlemen, I really don't like being asked all of these questions and I'm not at all sure that I wish to continue."

"Mr Chair, what you like and what you do is your concern – can you tell us where is the parish clerk?"

"There isn't one, I've never needed one."

"Mr Chair, you are obliged to have one."

"I've had enough of this and I close the meeting."

The following week, notices appeared on trees, buildings, railings, announcing an EXTRAORDINARY VILLAGE MEETING and asking residents to attend in the school hall. The three questioners tried to speak to the Council Chair, who refused any form of contact.

At the meeting, over three hundred people met and the situation of the moribund Council, its attitude, irregular behaviour and refusal to appoint a legal officer was aired. It was agreed that a council candidates list would be advertised, properly supervised elections held and an EGM of the village held to appoint a new Parish Council. Existing members of the Council would be eligible to submit themselves for election. The newly elected Council of nine members hired a clerk, Jeanette Styles, and lost no time in safeguarding the Old Pond. The pond, on its large irregular 'roundabout', was surrounded by tarmac and thereby now starved of rain run-off from the fields until it had become reduced to mud; and up came the weeds, long, strong, massed and formidable. The pond was going...

The building consortium helpfully suggested: "Fill it in, there's room there for four new executive properties."

At the last gasp, the new council found an energetic group of villagers who said: "No, it's our pond and it's going to remain our pond and just watch how good it's going to look."

Down came the old rickety posts for reconditioning and to give access to a long-armed digger – the roundabout was shut off (quite illegally) for two hours while eight tonnes of mud, silt, weeds and leaves were oh so carefully dredged and piled on the bank. In the new spirit, a local farmer had been persuaded – "Where d'you want it tipping?" – to donate a bowser of fresh water which was fed into the new hole so that the small fish, beetles and amphibians emerging from the banked mud could immediately return to their environment.

Pond group leader Gerry: "Now the bottom's clear we need clean old carpet – upside down we'll lay it all over the bottom to suppress weed regrowth and act as a cushion for the liner. Even before that, I've begged puddling clay so I need two volunteers for a very wet, muddy job."

Bette: "Yes, I'm on and my son Teddy."

"Thanks, Bette, Saturday, 9.30?"

"Will someone stick a card in the shop about the old carpet – thanks Rob, can we talk in a minute?"

They puddled, they carpeted, they butyl lined. It rained heavily and hey, there was five inches of real water in the Old Pond and they could see an occasional tiny fish.

Two more volunteers sidled up to Gerry one early morning.

"We used to have a pond before we moved here, I'm Geoff and this is Pat, would you like us to cut shelves under the top edge for water plants? Also, we've got about thirty that need a home that have been in pails – any use?

"Terrific, guys, yes to both please, any time you like for the ledges, can I show you the level they'll need to be?

"When do you expect water level up to final?"

"Prob in eight weeks, I've persuaded the Fire Dept to send up a tender for a bit of publicity and he'll give us 6,000 litres, which will be a help."

One of the new villagers had a dye works and in it were two wooden sheds.

"Gerry, they've been up twenty-odd years so the wood is mature – if you want to demolish and remove from site within five weeks from now, it's yours."

"Damien, that's very kind."

"No use to me, so glad to be of help. I'm also able to give you one trip with a flatbed."

"Great."

So for the cost of a wrecking bar and two claw hammers they had enough decent wood for their team leader Ian, the professional carpenter, to construct railings, a safe walkway for pushchairs and mums, an access gate and even a stable platform for children to peer into the pond (under supervision) at aquatics and flora and fish as the pond developed.

As the Old Pond's reputation grew lifebuoys appeared at both ends and two wonderful seats from tree trunks; shrubs, planted, hawthorns clipped, flowers multiplied and within five years the Old Pond had set itself fair for another century and for the pleasure of all ages.

THE CANDIDATES

In the typically English town of Broadhurst, it is almost local election time; Broadhurst has about eighty thousand citizens of whom roughly one in seven were not born there or thereabout and roughly one in twenty-seven have a pretence at some sort of religion. There are fifty-five councillors and all parties are deciding who their candidates in the elections will be.

Keeley Mason is twenty-nine, tall, brunette, sexy and divorced. She is a senior librarian and keen ten pin bowler with her own flat. Two men in particular are very interested in Keeley – Marson, a freelance brickie, so good at his trade that he can afford a top of the range BMW, and Gil, a local estate agent; both early thirties and both keen candidates.

St Veronica's is an academy with 1,400 pupils and a governing body of seventeen – currently they have one vacancy for a citizen governor and one for an academy nominated governor and have invited two candidates to meet a sub-committee of three governors for preliminary discussions – April, an NHS accountant and Brian, a milk roundsman for a national milk distributor.

Broadhurst CC is a famous cricket club dating from 1870 and running four elevens and two youth elevens – it has a committee of nine members with president ex officio. There are three vacancies currently – it is not necessary to be a player but a ratio of at least three players must be maintained. There are three candidates.

And so we can see many vacancies have arisen for quirky fate to fill! At Broadhurst CC AGM the three candidates were announced: April James whose father had played many years, was a member in her own right and a famed cake maker for cricket teas; Marson Wright, fast bowler and bricklayer who had built the toilet extensions at the club; Brian Deeley, leg spinner and milk roundsman; all elected by acclamation to the committee. April, in addition, was appointed and agreed to be the Treasurer.

Keeley Mason, in the meantime, was being avidly courted by her candidates – pop concert with Marson, cinema and dinner with Gil. Race meeting with Gil; weekend away with Marson.

When asked by her friend Louise: "Well, which one, or is there someone I don't know about yet, madam?" she calmly replied: "I don't need to vote yet – nothing to say, Mr Right hasn't appeared yet – they're both nice enough but…"

So the courting campaign rolls on.

Neither Brian Deeley nor April James, having been elected to the cricket club committee, are aware that they are also candidates to become governors at St Veronica's; so when Brian is shown into the waiting room at the school: "April, I don't believe it! Are you a candidate for the governors too?"

"Hello Brian, yes I am but I don't think we're rivals – we're in different categories of governor, you're the important one, you're a candidate as citizen governor."

"Yes, I know, I've been reading up on the differences and responsibilities – so it's possible we could both be on both – that's amazing."

"Yes, rather nice I think, you could teach all the board to bowl leg breaks."

"Don't think so, need big fingers."

After several hours of questioning and individual interviews by separate governor groups, they left, wondering.

Local selections for local elections took place in Broadhurst – Keeley's family had always worked for the council and voted Labour so when a Labour councillor who knew her father and had used her as a canvasser suggested she could be a candidate, she was quite excited. Her height and looks and ability to express herself impressed the agent enough for her to be adopted as the candidate for Hillside ward, adjacent to where she lived; and immediately leaflets were available –

"Hello, I'm Keeley, your Labour candidate, I hope you'll let me try to sort out your local problems – I only live over the back."

Two thousand doors later she was saying it in her sleep. Quite soon she began to run across Gil Vincent, local estate agent and Lib Dem candidate for the same ward.

His team were leafleting as enthusiastically as hers – they met on Harefield Road.

"Oh," said she. "I didn't know you were a candidate for my ward and my wardrobe – I'll have to think about this state of affairs."

"Well, then, madam, get used to it, I shall love you even more as I beat you out of sight."

"Rubbish," she said, "about beating, anyway, just give up now."

"Bosh!"

DAD'S DREAMS

Yes, honestly! When he was born his father, John Spearman, was so delighted to have a son, after goodness knows how many girl births in all branches of the family, that he determined to give him the most masculine name possible – Lance the Spearman. (He was talked out of 'the' by the registrar and so Lance Spearman he became.)

Luckily (or not) Lance had been an enormous fourteen pounds five ounces at birth, so Liz, his mother, understood how he was always going to be TOUGH in his father's eyes.

"I suppose he'll be heavyweight world boxing champ won't he, John?" she teased him when Lance was three months old – "Don't joke, Liz – he probably will be, look at those fists."

John bought him a set of barbells on his first birthday – suitable for an eighteen year old. "Just to get him used to weights."

In his cot, from birth, was a full-size cricket ball. He procured a beanie with a skull on it for Lance and was most put out to find him not wearing it at nursery.

As Lance advanced from babe to toddler, John each week believed his voice was on the point of breaking. "Can't you hear it, Liz, it's deeper this week?"

John took him to his own barbers and had his head shaved. Lance howled in his barbershop, all the way home and into Liz's arms.

"How dare you ruin his lovely hair, he's heartbroken."

"No, he's not, his hair wasn't manly, it's just a shock, he'll love it when he gets used to it – he doesn't want to be all softie, he wants to be well hard."

However much John wished and tried and imagined that his son was going to be a well-hard tough, by the time he had reached nursery, it was becoming clear to everyone except John that Lance was much more interested in girlie things. He loved playing with Liz's make-up, experimenting wearing her four-inch heels, trying on a fascinator she had hired for a wedding. Drawing endless pictures of little girls and lambs and angels at nursery – always using pink and pale pastel shades to colour with – much preferring to sit beside the classroom assistant at playtime rather than tear round the play area with the boys. Liz thought it marvellous that her son could be so gentle and creative compared with his father, who enjoyed headbutting bulldozers.

When Lance moved up to big school, it was plain that he was artistic, intelligent and not in any way effeminate although very disinterested in masculine activities that required overdoses of machismo. Would he be lucky enough to find teachers who understood what they had in Lance? With some encouragement from John (well one of his heroes, Bob Dylan, was a type of musician according to John) and a great deal of attention by Liz and her friend Celia Smyth, the music teacher, Lance had started learning the violin. His unusually large hands and long fingers for a six year old had made it quite a degree easier to cope with left-hand fingering and he made steady progress – practice, the bane of child learning, was no problem to Lance, he wanted to play his violin, so he practised. John, by this time beginning to realise that Lance was unlikely to be a lock forward, but might one day be a recognised fiddle player, boarded out the garage and fitted it with power lights and space heater so that Lance could practise whenever and for as long as... without driving everyone nuts. Of course he passed exams and exams – and Liz glowed and John didn't glower any more; until...

By age twelve, Lance had grown taller than Liz – he had appeared in concerts and his senior school were pleased to have a young student of such potential. A dance group at the school's leader, Pam Latimer, a top year student, said: "Lance, would you be willing to play practice for us – we would be really grateful?"

"Well Pam, I would like to help, when do you need me?"

"Lunchtime Thursdays and half nine on Saturdays for two hours."

"I'll need to check with my parents about weekends but it should be OK and lunchtime for sure."

"That's really cool Lance, thanks"

The dance group performed as five and as part of a much larger corps and Lance became a part of them. His music developed with and through this contact and rapidly became almost his whole learning compass.

At fifteen, Lance left secondary school to attend the music academy and at seventeen made his solo debut at Fairfield Halls in front of an audience of two thousand – his parents were astonished, his father perhaps, not least because he was wearing a pink shirt. He was offered a scholarship in Italy for two years and returned to his home only briefly in the years before his twenty-third birthday, by when he had studied in Italy, Germany, America and France as well as London.

He tried to explain: "I love ballet, I love the co-operation and integration of dance and music and my violin enables me to express that all powerful feeling."

They nodded, understanding he was a renowned violin player at least.

"Why do you have to muck around with that dancing when you're such a marvellous violin player; don't you just like being a soloist with the big orchestras?" John asked, not comprehending.

"Yes Dad, I do enjoy solo performing, I've been fortunate to be invited to work with them all in Russia, Germany, USA, England, Italy, China, everywhere, playing almost every major work for violin and with a lot of the maestri around today but my first love is ballet and I've hardly scratched the surface of what I want to do as a player, artistic director or even ballet composer."

"I'm sure you'll do quite wonderfully darling," Liz sighed, "and you cut all his hair off."

FEUD

It had begun a long time ago, the family feud.

"How did it start, Mum?" Diane asked Pat Dowson one Saturday morning when daughter and mother were having coffee in Mum's kitchen.

"I'm uncertain about the precise details but I believe it was at a family wedding in the 1890s, so over a hundred and twenty years ago, that the father of the bridegroom told the bride's brother that his cravat was inappropriate or some such nonsense. The bride's family forthwith gave the bridegroom a very hard married life and completely blanked his family."

"D'you mean the bride's family didn't speak to them?"

"Yes, I think the Lincoln family only spoke to John Farmer when absolutely necessary and never, ever had any communication with the Farmer clan, even though the two families lived about six miles apart."

"So how long did this last?"

"As best I can tell, it is still in force – because of marriage the names have multiplied, but your Uncle Peter did some genealogical research on the computer about four years ago and found seven or eight different surnames which he traced back to Farmer and Lincoln in 1898 in Westvale. Four on one side and four on Farmers'.'"

Diane said: "Lily Lincoln was the bride, wasn't she?"

"Yes, that was her name, poor woman, can you imagine, her mother making sure that the grandchildren, and I think there were six, spent as little time as possible with the parents of her daughter's husband."

"Absolutely ridiculous, d'you know anything else that happened?"

"Well, yes, a few things – Mrs Lincoln was the governor of a village school near where they lived and she refused admission to a little boy who was the child of the cook of the Farmer family; in the First World War, one of the nephews of the original Mr Farmer was a Major in the local county regiment and he refused to allow the promotion of a Second Lieutenant Newton who was a cousin of the Lincoln family, causing him to transfer to another regiment; when he was killed immediately after going to France, the Lincoln clan blamed it on the Farmers."

On the edge of the Cotswolds in a smart hotel, an assistant manager, Russell Mason, was chatting to his cousin Lincoln Piatt during his mid-shift break.

"I'm glad you chose to stay here Linc, I've not seen you in ages."

"Me too, quite by chance, actually, Aunt Heather told my Mum you were working here over a year ago and so it's been in the back of my mind, and I was due to be in London today, but my appointment cancelled so I turned right at Oxford and came here."

"What d'you want to drink?"

"Glass of Sauvignon please."

"Gus, two glasses of Bin 4 please – my account, thanks."

"Talking of Heather, she must be over eighty isn't she?"

"Yes, eighty-eight, I think, and going well."

"I remember talking to her at Matthew's wedding a long while back and she was telling me about the feud."

"Oh, God, the damned feud."

"Yes, that – apparently after the First World War, when one of the Lincolns, Jarvis, I think, had won the MC and been killed, his name was engraved on the big granite memorial in Laithburn together with his decoration and a couple of years later, the MC decoration after his name had been chiselled off. The Lincolns, of course, raised hell, blaming the Farmers, who had an auction house there, and it proved impossible to re-engrave it on, or to prove guilt. However, she told me that in 1922 or 1923 the auction rooms mysteriously burnt flat and no one was ever charged."

"It's really quite amazing how this dammed thing appears to have kept going. You and I are Lincolns, although neither of us has that surname. I read a piece in a magazine in the States a few years ago about a family called Tyler, with the mother's maiden name Farmer, living in Ann Arbor, Michigan (the mother had emigrated in the early 20th Century from the UK). They attracted the most extraordinary ill luck, over thirty to forty years, imaginable. Flocks of poultry dying for no reason, vehicle tyres slashed, vehicles bursting into flames, house fires, bicycle thefts, mail box vandalism, pets shot – eventually a man called Coleman had been apprehended and jailed who remained mute. He was also an immigrant. Coleman had been the family name of cousins of the Lincolns.

"I have a feeling," said Russell, "that the internet has made it very easy genealogically to maintain a trace on any family down the decades if you have that sort of mind."

"You're quite right," agreed Lincoln, "and if you're sick enough to want to feud, what could be simpler?"

"Just think," said Russell, "If it had all started forty years earlier there were an awful lot of Southern farmers didn't like Abraham Lincoln."

"Ouch, that's terrible."

Diane Dowson was the deputy head of a 3FE primary school and had nine years' experience as a teacher. Because of her enthusiasm and optimism, parents almost always liked and trusted her and her head, Jonathan Tryon, had not yet found a fault worth mentioning in the two years she had deputised for him. Kids flocked to her and learned discipline and knowledge. She had applied for the headship of a similar 3FE primary school on the retirement of the head and was shortlisted. Her remaining rival was twenty years older, female, without deputy experience and conservative in every possible regard. Those in the know considered Diane a shoo-in – both candidates were finally re-interviewed by four governors and the chair. Two old governors voted for the old candidate, two not old governors voted for Diane Dowson. Casting vote went to the chair, Mr Farmer – the old candidate was appointed.

HERRINGS BEQUEST

"Tell me, Grandad, about that will thing please."

"It's so long ago, you wouldn't be interested, Damien," said James Myers.

"I am, Grandad, ever since we were on holiday and my cousin Susan said there was a huge treasure in a will or something."

"Well, it all started just over a hundred years back, in 1908 actually, when your great-great-grandmother Matilda married a man called Linus Ogilvie on the other side of the world near Australia."

"Wow, that's a long way away, how old was she when she got married?"

"You've got right to the heart of it there Damien because Matilda Herring, yes, that was her name, was eighteen, nearly nineteen and she had been sent from her very wealthy family, the Herrings, in Norfolk, to live with some distant relations in Tasmania; d'you know where that is?"

"Yes, I do, it's that big island south of Australia."

"Exactly right – she was very pretty with dark hair and quite tall and she was a very good horsewoman, which was pretty useful because the Horsfalls had a huge estate in Tasmania and the only way to get around it was to ride. She went out there to be their heir because they had no kids. Pretty good, you might think."

"Ok, so far we've got Matilda marrying Linus – bad news for the Herrings in England and the Horsfalls in Tas – yes, bad news because she was supposed to land in Tasmania and marry a bloke that the Horsfalls had picked out for her; naughty, naughty Matilda. Worse yet, she married Linus on board the ship, a brig they were sailing on, and on which he was second mate. The marriage was conducted by the captain – yes, in those days the captain of a ship over a certain tonnage could legally marry people and issue a marriage certificate.

"Now things go from worse to dreadful – about a week after the marriage ceremony, in a violent storm, the ship is wrecked and only Matilda and four seamen, none of whom speak English, survive.

"In a whale-skin purse, her marriage licence survived with her, which was handy because shortly thereafter she discovered that she was 'with child'."

"Goodness Grandpa, what a story, what happened to her next?"

"Well, as you might imagine, it took some time for news of the disaster to reach the Horsfalls and it was decided that a pregnant distant relative was not welcome – so much for Christian charity. Her parents were utterly furious, ashamed and in no mood to welcome her either.

"They provided the minimum possible resources to bring her back to England with her child and her father interrogated her sternly, casting doubt that she had actually married. Crisis!

"Her father had reluctantly provided a thatched cottage on the estate for her, and when she went to fetch the whale-skin purse – it had disappeared!

"No marriage licence, no husband, no witnesses, no registrar – she was shamed and lived quietly the rest of her life in the cottage with Ben, her son.

"So furious had her grandfather been at the whole episode that he redrew his will so that 'no child born out of wedlock can take benefit from it'. As both of Matilda's siblings predeceased her, the whole estate has been locked in a closed trust ever since his death in 1912."

"Does that mean all that money is still locked up in what you just said?"

"Yes, exactly – because she couldn't prove that her child was born in wedlock, then the money can't be released to anyone directly in line from her child – that's Ben, and I'm Ben's son."

"Wow, Grandad, does anyone know how much is in that money mountain?"

"Well, yes, because the trust issues a statement – it's about forty-seven million pounds."

"Oh, my goodness."

"Yes, you could say that."

Damien was utterly fascinated by Grandad's saga – James Ogilvie, multi-millionaire, if only he could find... He knew Matilda's cottage very well; stone build, remnants of thatch, in the middle of a huge thicket of trees much taller than the ruins – on their land with a big sign 'Danger – Keep Out' since the last roof timbers crashed in over ten years ago. Matilda had lived there for twenty-eight years and he had never dared go near, but now...

Headline in the national press ten days later: 'Antique marriage licence found in ruins'.

MELANIE

Melanie was pretty, fair, petite and very determined – when Louis had succumbed to post-crash injuries six years before, her world had just imploded. They had done everything together.

Slowly she had come out of that dark area by concentrating on a future without him, but with her succeeding, as she had felt he would have wanted. New hairstyle, new colours, new clothes, new career; enrolled part-time computer planning, joined computer engineering company (at the bottom), sold their house and moved into a two-bedroom apartment which forced her to change nearly all her furniture. "It's not because I didn't love Louis and all we did," she told Jasmine, her cousin, "but I can't and won't live in the past. I'm thirty-six and my life didn't stop when his did and although I was very bitter that he was taken from me, bitterness is bloody useless, it just shrivels you. I'm going to succeed as I would have done if Louis and I had been together."

By her thirty-eighth birthday she had graduated, become a section head, joined a pottery class and met several men, all younger than she and all of whom were keen to pursue a longer relationship than she wanted. She had travelled on a couple of Eurostars to European holidays, one by train to Provence and one to Southern Brittany, but both involved quite tedious travel as she now had a morbid fear of flying, developed since Louis' death in his friend's Cessna 172.

Her renewed life had become dynamic and one day she realised that she had unconsciously become self-confident, driven, with a definite aim in mind – she was determined to become a director of a large commercial entity and was quite sure that she had the ability if not yet the experience to achieve.

One evening she had invited two girlfriends round to her place for supper, one with a boyfriend and one with her husband – although her dining room couldn't cope with a party of five, her patio could and she had an awning fixed over it when she bought the property with space heaters for 'iffy' nights. Fabia, one of the friends, rang her the day before and asked if she could 'be cheeky and bring a friend as well as my husband'.

Melanie thought, patio, no problem.

"Sure, look forward to seeing you all tomorrow."

Following day, she was so frantic in the office that she almost missed getting to the butcher for the double ribs she had ordered but just made it and just home and just about everything before the bell pinged exactly 8pm.

First up, Georgina and boyfriend Fred, whom she knew, kisses, chocs, wine, thanks, help yourself, how nice and all that; 8.10 Fabia and Luc and oh my goodness, she was expecting a girlfriend and here was 'paradise in pants' called Michael; more wine and chocs and flowers (from Michael) an orchid, (how did he know she adored orchids?) and hugs and all that good stuff. Fabia knew Georgina, they both knew Melanie and all the girls were backless and almost topless and short. I mean short and on five-inch spikes and looking 'heaven' and hungry – for what – well, indeed, for what?

The boys just happened to hunk about and some of the tan may have been real.

Supper was a party and Melanie normally kept twenty-five plus bottles of wine around and by 1am there wasn't too much left.

Luc had so many wicked stories in so many good accents and Michael had been to a lot of places. Georgina clearly thought Luc entirely wonderful and Fred certainly didn't dislike Melanie too much, although Melanie also got some positive echo from Michael. Come 1am she suggested they might all want to sleep somewhere else and with expressions of undying friendship, off they went.

Mid next morning, and feeling maybe a touch detached, a call came in.

"Hi Melanie, Michael – morning, two things – thanks for last night and giving you tonight to get some rest, may I take you to dinner, 8.30 on Thursday – perhaps at Petrarch's?"

Quite surprised but on the case: "Michael, thank you, yes I enjoyed it too – may I check my diary? If you'd like to call me after lunch, I'll know how I'm fixed, OK. Bye for just now."

Round one to Melanie. Of course he re-called – she agreed 8pm Friday; round two to Melanie.

The girls were keen to follow up.

"Hi Melanie, Fabia, did Michael contact you? – he seemed smitten and so did you, sweetie."

"Yep, we had dinner at Petrarch's on Friday, but that's all."

"You mean that's all you said yes to – so far."

"Whatever."

"Keep me posted."

"There may not be anything."

"Yeah, right."

"Georgina, Mel, has he proposed yet?"

"Ha ha ha, not funny – we've had dinner; that's it. How's Luc babe? – Better be careful."

"Yeah, I think I had way too much, I got such an earful from the master!"

"I'm not surprised – see you soon."

However, Michael and Melanie met again on the Sunday and Tuesday and she found he was a ferry pilot working for a number of companies over Europe and sometimes further. He had a share in a Piper PA 31 aircraft in which he sometimes flew smart parties commercially around the UK. Having told him of her dread of flying he quietly told her: "I can cure that for you, when the time is right."

They found very quickly that they were a natural pair – food, decor, travel, films, sport – and moved into each other's lives quietly and naturally. One Saturday lunchtime they went out to Shipston-on-Stour and over lunch opened a couple of bottles of wine. Melanie did not notice that Michael hardly drank his glass and disposed of it whilst she was looking elsewhere, while she, relaxed and enjoying herself, drank well over a bottle of Crozes-Hermitage in the two hours they were at the table. Over coffee in the lounge she accepted a liqueur so that when they got back in the car she was very warm, relaxed and sleepy.

He suggested: "I think we'll just slip up the 429 to Wellesbourne and have a look at my plane."

"Lovely darling."

Twenty minutes later, parked safely, Michael unlocked his Piper, taxied out, registered a local flight with the control tower and woke Melanie up.

"Here we are darling, there's my old bus, ready to go, fancy a little trip over the pub we've just lunched in?"

"Why not?"

So in they got and off they took and as Michael knew perfectly well, alcohol nearly always removes the fear of flying because it relaxes reactions and perceptions. After twenty minutes they landed. Melanie:

59

"That was so pretty, what a lovely way to end lunch."

And so three months later, when they took off to fly to Mauritius on their honeymoon, Melanie had drunk several large glasses two hours before check in. Who was afraid of flying?

NICOLA'S CONTRAPTION

"Well," she said to her great friend, Moo. "I'm not sure where I got it, or when, but it's given me hours of fun and it's very reliable and as you know, it's so convenient."

Nicola was married with two children, Billie and Blue. Billie's real name was Mary Frances and Blue properly should have been called Helen – Nicola, as usual, couldn't quite remember why they had such strange nicknames, and her partner, Jake, had only ever known them as Billie and Blue.

Nicola was thirty four, dark red haired, angular and slender and a part-time music teacher of violin and piano. The children's father, Martin, had decided to preach and teach in Mongolia for reasons he had not explained and had not been heard from for more than nine years. On the presumption of desertion, Nicola had made appropriate decisions, with the full support of parents and in-laws, to both of whom she was closely linked.

"I'm going, today actually, over to Ringswold to that art exhibition because Jane Mere has got some stuff showing – d'you want to come?"

"Are you biking?"

"Yes, of course, it's only six miles and on the contraption it will take thirty five minutes max."

"Yes, OK, can my two share your mum with your two?"

"Yep, of course, I'll call her to say; half eleven suit you, here?"

"Perfect, see you then."

The contraption was a dark green, iron framed, Indies model, three-geared bicycle built approximately thirty five years before. It had Sturmey Archer gears, Ransom lights, a sprung saddle that would have not been out of place on a tractor, chain guard and wide solid tyres, quite impervious to anything except landmines or earthquakes. It might have been a familiar sight to cowboys in Texas as its wide handlebars resembled the huge horns on Western Longhorn cattle; Nicola's however were complete with bell and bell-shaped hooter.

By a simple, central, drop bolt the whole contraption could be folded in half against itself, once basket and saddle bag had been removed. Imagine a folding, riding, ten tonne contraption – awesome!

Moo and Nicola met at the village cross and set off for Ringswold – Moo:

"Can I put this case in your front basket, pal?"

"Sure, what's in it?"

"A puppy – our dog dropped six, two months ago if you remember and we've sold five, and this is the last, which has been bought by an old lady in Ringswold, so I thought I'd deliver it today via your contraption."

"Sure, good idea, I've got the only basket big enough to carry a cow never mind a puppy in its second month. Isn't your bitch a Cocker spaniel?"

"Yes, thought the same, how an old lady will cope with a volcano on springs called puppy, I can't imagine, but she came to see him and was quite sure."

"How much did you get for the litter, if you don't mind me asking?"

"I don't mind at all, £800 for the first four and £1,000 for the two last."

"Why the difference?"

"Because of scarcity or I told her she could have the pick of next year's litter."

"What price will that be?"

"Not sure, but certainly over £1,000 each because this litter has been so brilliant."

"Oh, did I mention carriage charge for pedigree Cockers is £25 per mile?"

"You can…"

The contraption went at a steady speed, not much above twenty mph on the level with Nicola in the saddle; Sir Chris Hoy might have got it up to forty, downwind. The solid tyres didn't mind potholes but the rims recorded them with numerous nicks, jags and distortions which because they were solid, let no air escape. Moo was able to dawdle her modern machine and enjoy conversation, scenery and the gentle exercise.

On one stretch, past Dunfield Church, they were overtaken by a peloton of enthusiastic male riders, kitted, helmeted and synchronised – various semi-humorous comments floated back.

"Rear brake stuck darling?" "Walk babe, it's quicker." "Need a tow?" Nicola: "Silly sweaty boys."

The contraption ground ever onward and later, Moo swore remembering them overtaking a snail – just.

They reached the art display; as usual a large proportion pretty average but one or two really interesting pieces. Moo wanted to buy a miniature five inch by six inch study of an oak tree, in oils; the price by a signed but unknown artist was too rich at £375.

Nicola, perhaps out of loyalty, was fascinated by an agglomeration of bicycles leaning against a corrugated shack in a delightful range of ochre and brick and grey shades. The artist was one of the curators of the show and he and Nicola came to an agreement; she would lend him the CONTRAPTION for a whole day as a subject and she would purchase his Cycles Collection for £125, a reduction of £75. As well: "Well, all right, I will put the world contraption somewhere on the painting – where my signature goes."

"Wow, fame at last. 'Nicola's Contraption' or perhaps even 'Nicola's Velocipede'.

Over the rest of the summer, Nicola, Moo and their friends and families barbecued, partied, met, chatted, gardened and decided late in July that it would be fun to have a really huge picnic on Halliday's Meadow. The meadow had been used for picnics as far back as village memories went. It had never been ploughed because it really wasn't suitable; a stream wandered across it, just deep enough never to dry out on its way to feed Fowlers Pond in the middle of the meadow; Fowlers Pond wasn't more than three feet deep but ducks loved it and, therefore, ducklings and a family of moorhens lived in the reeds; and there were two wonderful specimen trees, one in the middle of half of the meadow, an oak, at least three hundred years old, and the other a horse chestnut over ninety feet high had been persuaded to grow one huge limb beside Fowlers Pond so that generations had been able to swing, dive, jump or tumble from it into the cool waters below – WONDERFUL!

The picnic planning was just fun! Moo elected boss: "Ok then – Jane, sausages please, 250, OK?"

"Cripes, are you sure?"

"More do you think?"

"I'm thinking much less."

"Well, I don't want to start riots but if everyone's going to query everything we're going nowhere – so Jane, 250, OK?"

"Sorry, of course."

"Leanne, green salad please, can you base it on 30 long lettuces and five kilos of tomatoes?"

"No probs, boss."

"Nicola, will you buy, soak and roast six gammon joints and get them sliced; May's got an electric slicer."

"Sure, no problem."

"May will you borrow six or eight biggish cold bags and get two five-kilo or five two-kilo boxes of ice cream to go in them on the morning of the picnic."

"Who will calculate and get the number of rolls we will need – thanks Lara – don't forget any gluten free."

"Boiled eggs anyone? Thanks Joy" and on and on.

"Linda, will you be treasurer, if everyone who is coming with kids gives you £20 then if everyone who buys anything for the picnic gives you the receipt you can reimburse them – whatever's over, spend on wine, OK?"

Leanne suggested: "Shall I get Tim to go round begging beer, booze, balbec and blemonade?"

"Marvellous – now as the men are on a freebie so far, which of them are going to be safety wardens for the tree and pond – cos if we don't, need I say more?"

Two of the girls volunteered to get a small roster of a few men covering the whole afternoon with appropriate ropes and poles.

The afternoon arrived, with tables covered by every sort of pie, tart, quiche, ham, salmon, salad, egg, rolls, desserts, soft drinks, water, beer, wine. Families arrived by car, on foot, by cycle and on the now famous CONTRAPTION.

The new painting had featured in the local paper and everyone had clamoured for Nicola to ride it into Halliday's Meadow and down to Fowlers Pond – she did, to loud applause. Pedalling bravely, straining girlfully she reached five feet from the edge and, without warning, the retaining bolt flew up, the contraption folded and poor Nicola executed a beautiful, extended swallow dive right into Fowlers Pond!

THE STRAWBERRY PICKERS

"I just wish you'd do something instead of loafing around looking spare -that is when you bother to get up at all," – father to teenage son. Common enough. Lynton to Jonny in this farm; a hundred and ninety five acres arable, about the same pasture, not very good grass so more needed for the Holstein herd. Lynton's Dad, Felix, still around sometimes; always helpful, careful not to poke his nose in what is now Lynton's farm. Jonny, pleasant but not urgent about anything; OK results GCSE now waiting for repeat A level Doomsday; three more weeks. "I'm sure he's done very nicely, Lyn." Mum Glenys was sure of nothing of the sort but maybe good wishes could help.

Brainwave – 8am next morning: "Jonny, down here please, I need to talk, now."

"Goodness Lyn, he'll have a heart attack."

"I've got an idea for him, that just might ignite his mighty brain. Oh, good morning Jonny, cup of coffee?"

"No thanks, Dad, I'm in a state of shock, what did that bellow just now mean?"

"It meant, my dear son, that I want you to come with me, right after breakfast, to look at something very exciting."

"What is it?"

"Come and see; are you having something to eat or drink?"

"I think you should Jonny."

"No, thanks, Mum, I'm ready."

"OK, let's go."

They climbed in and on the Matbro and lumbered off across the farm.

"Where are we off?"

"Vale End."

What's there?"

"Nothing."

"So why are we going there?"

"Wait ten minutes and I'll explain."

Vale End was a two and a half acre flat, sandy bottom surrounded by gullies, ditches, thickets and on one side a railway embankment.

It had never been considered crop-viable because of the difficulty in getting large units access there to plough or harvest, and it was not one large piece but several smaller areas semi-separated by gullies and ditches. When they arrived, Jonny switched off. His father: "Here's where we are, you're eighteen, earning nothing, costing me and your mother lots – you've not indicated even once any possible future career path, education course or interest. That stops now; you've had to repeat your A levels, I really do not care what those results will be. I do care that you start earning your keep. So – this is just over two acres of sandy soil, properly tilled it will grow strawberries, millions of them and strawberries make a lot of money. You are going to rotavate this soil because we can't get a tractor and plough here, fertilise it, straw it and plant strawberry plants, probably two thousand of them. We will put wire on this end of the field and a gate and a shed – when the fruit is ripe, we will advertise and you will be in charge of weighing and collecting the money -1 will pay for the costs and you and I will split the gross returns 50-50. How d'you like that?"

"I hate it."

"I thought you would, you've got until 6pm tomorrow night to agree, wholeheartedly, or find yourself other lodgings. You are eighteen and an adult – grow up."

Glenys had seen her husband's growing exasperation and although shocked at the ultimatum, sided with Lynton – she hoped Jonny wouldn't whinge to her – he didn't. At breakfast next morning, Jonny was down, laid the table and said to his parents: "Sorry I've been selfish, thanks for the opportunity, I'll start today, if you'll tell me what to do first." Both Glenys and Lynton were speechless – the family, for the first time, actually was a family in every sense.

Over the next three months, Jonny (and friends) with much guidance and help from Lynton and Granddad Felix and two days of professional labour, put over one and a half acres of land, long fallow, into cultivation and planted hundreds upon hundreds of rows of strawberries.

By mid-June adverts 'Famous Vale End Strawberries' appeared and the opening date – the shed was up with chair and counter and sole in/out gate And they came – Gwyneth and Charles at Letcoll House had a house party that weekend – "Charles, wouldn't it be fun if we all went strawberrying this afternoon – rough old clothes and trainers, we could probably eat our own weight?"

"Don't be daft, no one would want that."

"I bet they would, I'm going to find out."

And Gwyneth was right, four couples opted to go.

"Never had such fun." "Not been since I was a kid." "I'm absolutely filthy." "Gosh, I'm red all over." "How much have you picked?" And on and on. The whole lot of them were shrieking with laughter, the heat, the luscious smell, George fell over on his back, they were all sticky; when they got to Jonny to pay, Peregrine insisted on giving him £50 note.

"Hope that'll cover it, marvellous fun, thanks."

Nominally, you paid £5 for a jumbo empty punnet and kept the punnet and as many strawberries as you could cram into it. The best bets for Jonny were the families of Mum, Dad and three smallish kids – although the parents sensibly opted for three punnets, the squabbles of the children often meant them buying two more to restore peace and small children didn't fill punnets and didn't really get much beyond making a mess.

An elderly vicar and his sister arrived in an immaculate Austin Hampshire and after spending fifteen minutes contemplating the queue to the entrance, then had an enjoyable neo-theological debate as to whether one or two punnets were their predestined burdens. Having decided in favour of two, they were to be observed over the next two hours endlessly comparing the merits of individual berries before placing a favoured specimen occasionally in one or other. When finally they exited it could have been noted that in total their strawberries did not exceed twenty-five.

After Jonny had been there about four hours and he was incredulously realising that he had already taken in excess of £440, a hullaballoo was to be heard which rapidly increased in volume as it approached. A woman of perhaps late thirties appeared, surrounded and followed by what can only be described as a tribe.

As it reached the barrier, Jonny had the feeling of being captured by an incoming tide. The woman shouted: "Be still the lot o' yers," and certainly the volume for a moment decreased by perhaps two decibels – then uproar returned. There were nine, on the counter, on the shed roof, up the road, on each other – sheer, stark chaos personified. Just astern Attila's horse, a large, tall man, hairy-armed and hairy-faced, had had enough in two minutes flat; he gently tapped the woman's arm and said: "With your permission? SHUUUUUUT UPPPPP!!!!" at a vocal power that may not have been heard by the captain of a 747 flying overhead at 36,0000 feet. Everyone in Vale End picking berries stopped, camels chomping hay in London Zoo ceased, and the dreaded horde of nine froze – then he went on: "Your ma is here to see me this afternoon, so don't move unless she or I say so – each of you come and stand in line here, eldest on the right."

"Is that all right, Mrs?" he whispered.

"It's bloody marvellous," she said.

Jonny asked: "How many punnets please, ma'am?" The giant answered:

"Eleven please, one for the lady, nine for them and one for me, I'm paying."

"Right, now come here, you, the eldest, for your punnet, what's your name?"

"Now."

"I said, what's your name?"

"I told you sir, that's me name, Now."

"Right, come here next child, what's your name?"

"Now, sir."

"Hold on, are you saying you've the same name as your brother?"

"Yes sir, all of us six boys and tree girls are all called Now."

The man turned to the woman. "This is a very strange thing, ma'am, all your children called the same name and that name being 'Now'."

"Well," said she. "It's quite simple, whenever I want them, I open the back door and shout 'Get in Now[1]'."

Jonny was intrigued by this but realised that the horde together could not be supervised and would certainly either wreck or strip his fruit farm. The giant and the woman agreed on payment of an extra punnet, that he would take the eldest four and she would take the youngest five after a delay of twenty minutes. The result – nine very red Indians.

A police car arrived with four officers – two got out to negotiate. "How much for forty punnets please?"

Quick as you like: "£260 picked, £200 p.y.o."

"Ok, here's the £200 when can we start?"

"Now."

The police car departed, leaving two off-duty coppers, shortly joined by another four. One of them in his own van – when it departed over three hours later, full of full punnets, Jonny couldn't resist it: "I never thought I'd see eight officers caught in the act, red handed."

Late in the afternoon, a specially adapted car pulled in and the mechanism slowly placed an electric wheeled appliance down – the driver was a considerably aged woman and the car driver her husband, not any younger. Slowly, they reached Jonny and in some disappointment asked: "Don't you have any full punnets, then?"

"No, I'm sorry, we advertise Pick Your Own, so we don't."

Then an idea struck him. "Are you in a hurry?"

"No, not particularly, why?"

"Well, I think I may be able to help."

Jonny asked the next ten visitors if they would mind paying £4 for a full punnet and he would take a small amount from each to put into two punnets for the folk who were unable to pick for themselves – no one objected. He refused payment from the not quite fully able couple, who nevertheless gave him £10 for Cancer Research, the 'giver' customers felt pretty pleased as well.

Quite amazing really, how a random idea from his Dad triggered an unlikely response from Jonny, leading to a huge experience with all manner of fellow citizens he

would not have had; a chance to value labour with money
and perhaps a start for him as a man.